This book belongs to

....

ISBN 978-1-64638-182-1

www.cottagedoorpress.com

I Spy with My Little Eye

HALLOWEEN
HAUNT & FIND

cottage door press

Written by Rosa Von Feder
Illustrated by Nila Aye

This little ghost has got
to scurry ...

and find his
friends in a
big hurry!

Find and follow the
black kitten on every page.

The bright flash of
a lightning bolt

ALGEBRA MONSTERS Robots PHYSICS SWAMPS

FORCES VOLTAGES

Where is the frog?

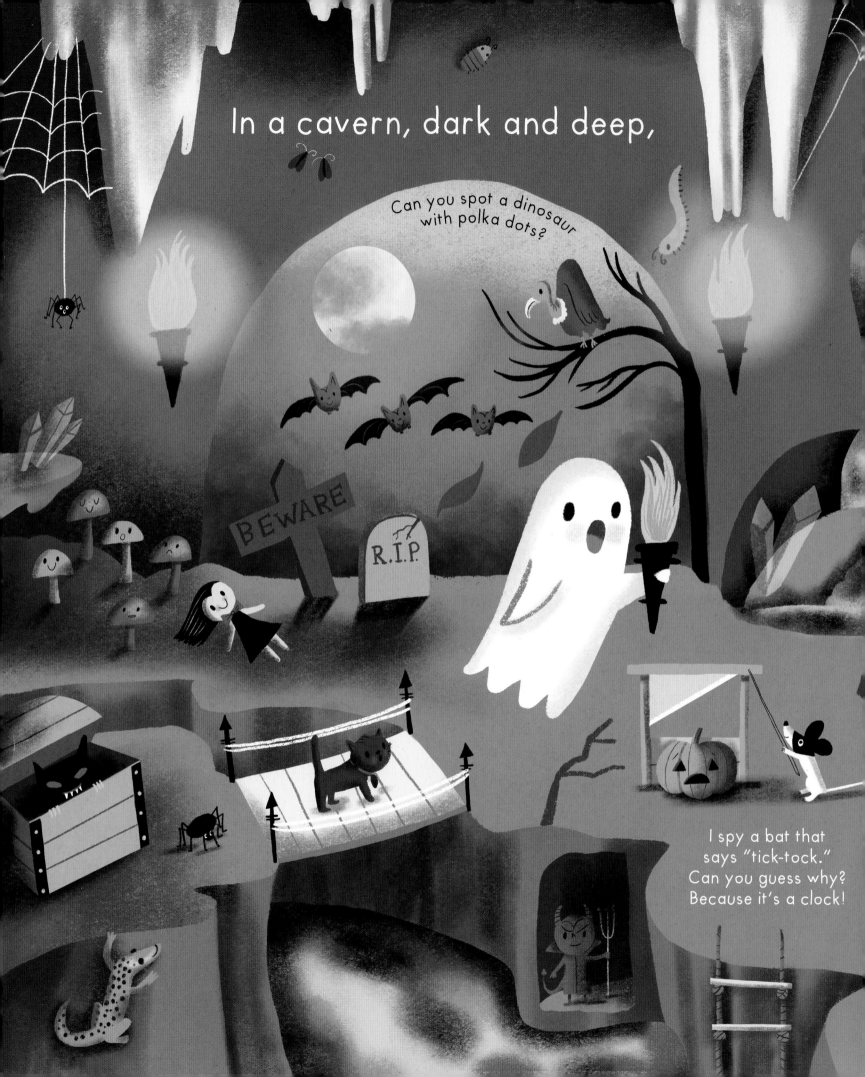

In a cavern, dark and deep,

Can you spot a dinosaur with polka dots?

BEWARE

R.I.P.

I spy a bat that says "tick-tock." Can you guess why? Because it's a clock!

2 vampires awake from sleep.

hang in there!

FIDO

I spy a walrus in a hat.
How 'bout you?
Can you find that?

Where did my doll go?

Can you count 7
pink mushrooms?

3 swamp creatures on a boat,

Can you spot
a stripy sock?

NO SWIMMING

fish for supper as they float.

Do you see 2 angry turtles?

Find 3 bottles.

I spy 4 ants.
Can you spot them, too?

4 helpful scarecrows point the way.

Can you count 3 pink mice?

Find the pig wearing a mask.

Up on their brooms, **5** witches fly

Can you count 3 magic spell books?

Vanishing SPELLS

SPELLS *for* LOVE

Hoot, hoot! Can you find 2 owls?

6 mummies tangled up in knots,

I spy 3 things —
red, pink, and blue.
Do you spot the
balloons, too?

Find the suit of armor.

dance the cha-cha and foxtrot.

Can you spot a scorpion?

Do you see 2 dancing mice?

Underneath the glowing moon,

Quack, quack!
Do you see a duck?

Where is the bunny?

In the darkest closet stirs

I spy a sweater with a cat.
How 'bout you?
Can you spot that?

Can you find 2 tennis rackets?

8 mischievous monsters!

Where is the red boxing glove?

Can you count 7 clothes hangers?

I spy something blue and slimy
reaching out of something shiny.
Can you spot 2 tentacles?

the SKeleton CREW

R.I.P. DEE COMPOSE

JACK O' LANTERN

1733 BARRY MEDEEP

Performing their groundbreaking work,

don't take kindly to outsiders.

Hooray, it's time to trick-or-treat
up and down the spooky street!

Where is the
orange cat?

Find the red bird.

Do you see a dog dressed like a bumblebee?

Can you find someone dressed like a hot dog?

Can you spy a green witch?

I spy something pink that squirms.
Can you count 8 wiggly worms?

THE END